**sharon darrow**

CANDLEWICK PRESS
CAMBRIDGE, MASSACHUSETTS

Copyright © 2006 by Sharon Darrow

First edition 2006

Library of Congress Cataloging-in-Publication Data is available.

Library of Congress Catalog Card Number 2006040618

ISBN-13: 978-0-7636-2624-2
ISBN-10: 0-7636-2624-4

2 4 6 8 10 9 7 5 3 1

Printed in the United States of America

This book was typeset in NewsGothic.

Candlewick Press
2067 Massachusetts Avenue
Cambridge, Massachusetts 02140

visit us at www.candlewick.com

For the Foos: Esther Hershenhorn, Franny Billingsley, Myra Sanderman, Carolyn Crimi, Esme Codell, & Laura Ruby, with love and gratitude

*Vernal, Arkansas, Sissy Lexie, age 16*

Garbage

I hate
how

we breathe it
    wear it
        stain our hands with it
        smell of it


Our boots & overalls
    Aunt Lannie's long dresses
    streaked with it

    (her religion won't let her wear pants)


Uncle Daddy drives the pickup
past a row of cans, downwind

    always downwind


Boy & me knock off the lids
lift the cans up to Aunt Lannie

standing on the heap
in wading boots, bandanna
over her nose

She empties them into the trailer
chucks them at my brother
& me & we slam

lids back on
Rowed up neat
empty they sit

Sour air hangs in the road
after we drive on

Each summer day is like the one before—
hot sun    blue sky    the truck    the trash    the stink—
each nighttime's harvest load of life's a bore.

Each minute's tick takes hours I can't ignore.
My eyes fill up & I try hard to blink
away this summer's tears. Like days before

I want to dream away the stench & gore.
I have to turn my brain off & not think
of night's gross harvest load, a lifeless bore.

I wake & sleep & breathe what I abhor,
the spoiled food & curdled milk. I shrink
from one more rotten day like those before—

old moldy bread, an oozing apple core,
green iridescent meat & maggot stink
blow through this summer day worse than before,
tonight, time's hardest load, this lifelong chore.

When we moved in,
Lannie Kate Fowler
      said:

            "Call me Aunt Lannie—
                  I ain't trying to take
                  your mama's place."

      said:

            "You can call Bobby Ray
            'Uncle Daddy' since you
            don't got one of your own—
            besides I call him Daddy,
            have ever since we lost
            our first little 'un."

      said:

            "I'm calling you 'Bo.'
            'Boy' don't ring
            right in my ears.
            What kind of mama
            don't bother to name
            a son?"

      said:

            "Your mama might come back
            someday, dearie, mark
                  my words—
                  my word!—
            what kind of mama
            ups & leaves
                  a girl
                  like
            you?"

Once I asked Mama:
"Why'd you name us Sissy & Boy?"

At school, kids laughed at us,
said she'd used up every name
she knew & every man, too,

on our brothers & sisters      or
never got around to it      or
was too darn lazy      or

But she said:
"Would you rather be Number Six & Number Seven?"

Our mama was always giving us up

to the Welfare people & taking off,

till Children's Services told her only

one     more     chance     before she'd lose us for good.

Our big sister Raynell & her husband,

Jobe, took us in, but when hard times hit them

& Mama heard, she up & absconded

with herself, sold our old house, everyone

else all growed up & —— gone.

Hard to believe now, but

every time she gave us up

I cried at night, missing Mama—

her rough voice gravelly,
her cigarettes glowing
in the dark—

her rocking in a straight chair
& humming lullabies
when she thought we slept.

Life was good when

> we lived with Raynell & Jobe in Vernal,
> walked five blocks to middle school
> (Boy in sixth grade & me in eighth),
> had art classes for the first time
> & went home at lunch,
>
> then Baby Kylie came,
> Jobe lost his job,
> they lost their house,
> & we all moved

back out to Lexieville,
in with Jobe's dad,
Jobe's mama dead & gone.
Our house sold & gone,
all of us squeezed
into two rooms
all summer, squeezed up
& sweating, Kylie
screaming her little head off.
Her screaming gave
us all a sick headache

till Jobe's daddy talked to a neighbor lady, name of Lorelei,

& she let Boy & me sleep over there
at night. School bus stopped right outside her door,
  took me to senior high, Boy to junior high.
  Boy quit
  doing homework, did nothing
  but draw rockets & robots.

  One night Boy got up to mischief.

  Next day the junior high lockers gleamed with black

  painted robocopters

      & school expelled him

& me,
said I aided & abetted,
but I didn't know a thing about it.
Why would I want us to get sent away from Raynell?

& why would Boy?  I asked him & made him cry.
Welfare placed us back in Vernal
with Mrs. Clay, a retired art teacher.
At first, I stayed mad at Boy &

cried at night,

missing Raynell,             but in art class,

Boy painted wall murals
& I covered benches with mosaics
made out of tiles      smashed      with a hammer.

We ate good & slept warm &
once we got to know her,
& Boy & I made up,
the three of us
laughed a lot at the stories
she told about art school, then

oh, Lordy,

Mrs. Clay had a stroke (scared Boy & me half to death).
She couldn't even talk,        just blinked at us,
& got moved to a rest          home near her daughter
& grandkids in Mablevale.      When we asked
could we visit her,            her daughter
& grandkids just               frowned.
I figured                      Boy & me
had no luck                    at all
when

we ended up in a trailer
    on the outskirts of Vernal
        with Sam, an old Cherokee guy,

& his son, Lou, in a wheelchair,
    we were supposed to help
        cook for & so on.

Lou taught Boy & me to bead
    belt buckles & hair clips
        we sold at flea markets

all summer long. After the first
    shock, we liked living there fine.
        Turned out Lou knew about

a million jokes & his daddy laughed
    no matter how many times
        he told them. I couldn't help

but think that was a fine way
    for a father to be,
        then school started

& what with no time left for homework,
    our social worker sent us
        away to where

Lannie & Bobby Ray Fowler live,    down Old Valley Cut-off,
close to the dump below Vernal,    a long bus ride to town.

A sign in their yard says:    RURAL TRASH
COLLECTION SERVICES.    But no need for reading—

I smelled it before I saw it.    They moved us in,
gave us our own rooms,    & set down all the ground rules.

I tried not to breathe.    Lannie caught me & said,
"Don't worry,    you'll get used to it."

I shut my windows    fast, but it didn't help.
From that minute on I knew,    no way could it get worse.

But on the school bus,    all the kids held their noses
& it got a lot worse.    We had to go anyway—

Boy in eighth, me in tenth &    we've been stuck here
a whole year—    so far.

Uncle Daddy-trash-man says
he knows
   all about Lexieville
     & Lexies


Uncle Daddy says
he knows
   Boy & me, we
     liable
       to rob him
        blind


He don't like nobody
   but Lannie, don't
     cotton to nobody
      else

Memories:

Whispering into the hall phone at midnight,
Begging Raynell, "Come get us!"

Uncle Daddy hollering about ground rules.
"No calls without permission."

Raynell & Jobe driving up, Lannie calling the police.
Boy & me mad as heck & scared, but we don't say so.

Next day Raynell made an official petition
But Welfare wouldn't let us go.

Welfare said Raynell could call once a week

Sometimes we got permission to visit
& we'd take a picnic out to DeGray
& swim till we turned into a crazy
bunch of laughing prunes
                              Boy & me painted
cartoons for Kylie & Raynell hugged us
& got teary-eyed
                              To this day nothing's
better than a big sister like Raynell
the way she makes even the worst old place
seem like a home filled with flowers
                              I wish
I could be a cozy home-feeling sister
to Boy like Raynell
                              But I don't know how

At first we thought we'd died & gone to hell, the smells,
rotten squishy stuff, who knows what, & Uncle Daddy
just cruising up there in his A/C-cooled truck cab

while we breathed in all the death for miles around.
We couldn't eat breakfast or we'd retch it up
all day. Eating was best at night after we bathed

off the stink & scrubbed the taste back into our mouths.
Lannie acted like every trailer load held treasure
& shuffled through it in her hip waders waving

a metal detector, in case somebody stupid had thrown
away their fortune & she'd be lucky enough to find it.
She'd dive right in, tried to get me to help, but

that was where I drew my line, though Uncle Daddy
made Boy wade in more than once. Flea market cash
was the object of the game. Lannie dug up junk people

thought was special, a collectible or antique like on eBay.
She loved Flea Market Mondays over to Benton Fair Grounds.
Maybe the stink made *me* crazy. I found treasures in the trash

myself. My game was to hide them from Lannie, to keep them
safe from the Fleas. I imagined owners ransacking dark houses
in search of a broken neck chain, a silver ring so tiny only

a fairy child could wear it, barrettes some mama had sewed
ribbons & lace on. Lots of valuable things are still valuable
after being trash. Once I discovered somebody's broken cell

phone & took it apart.  Boy called me a kook like Lannie
so I kept my finds secret, until I found a clay woman,
about the size of my thumb & ugly as sin in a cigar box

filled with little brushes & watercolors, squashed & rolled,
still good. "Look here, Boy. Want these?" He said, "Thanks!"
& for a minute there in the garbage, we were happy.

this week Raynell
calls to say
Jobe's sister's hired

him to paint
for her decoration
company in North

Little Rock, Arkansas,
where she does
rich people's houses

in the latest
styles, fabrics, paint,
wallpaper, accessories,

& fake fireplaces.
Boy & me
don't sleep good

now, Raynell going
away, leaving us
alone, missing her

Uncle Daddy's pickup

gleams bluish green metallic
gleams chrome

has A/C & stereo CD


in the cool of a morning
he opens the windows

his country & western
his Bible tapes

fill the air
we pass through

behind him
Lannie balances on the heap inside the trailer
Boy & me cling to the splintery top rail, gloves
slippery with garbage slime, boot
toes on the bottom rail
ready to leap for the next driveway

rusty metal trailer holds its bulging wooden sides
the way I try to hold my breath

in the poison midsummer
heat, garbage steams under my feet
biting flies swarm my face

Uncle Daddy's windows slide

shut & just

tire crunch
on gravel               &          cicadas'
                                    hot rattle

When Uncle Daddy yells
we scatter, but he never
raises a hand to us. *Just
don't steal nothing,* Lannie
whispers, or we'll soon
know the wrath
                    of the hand
                    of the Lord.

(asleep)

*in my own dream-*

*dark I glide over*

*pine tops   sift through needles*

*shape-shift   ghostly*

*nightmare rain*

(half-waking)

stale house   breathing

footsteps?   door opens

(awake)

one eye   watching me

What comes up missing:

his almanac—
    must have misplaced it, Lannie says (he stomps the floor)
his Jolene Durham CD—
      look under the truck seat, she says (he yells—we hide)
his mother-of-pearl pocketknife—
       (no stomping   no yelling   hand of wrath descends)


      on Boy's head

I heard him sobbing & crept in to say good night.
His gritty knuckles gripping his pillow tight,
Boy could hardly speak
when I patted on his head.

His gritty knuckles gripped his pillow tight.
I wept with him
as I patted on his head.
Boy whispered, "Don't let him hurt you, too."

I wept for him
back in my dark bed.
Boy warned me not to let him hurt me, too,
then he ran into the night.

Back in my dark bed
I didn't hear him leave
when he ran into the night.
Now he's all alone.

I didn't hear him leave.
Boy could hardly speak.
Now he's all alone,
crying & creeping through the night.

he took nothing
except his backpack
notebooks & pens

loaf of bread
& peanut butter
from lannie's kitchen

uncle daddy searches
boy's room   no
pocketknife   imagine

boy wandering swamps
in fog   sleeping
exhausted & unprotected

dear lord   close
the crocodile's mouth
keep boy safe

doodles & scrolls & squiggles
squirrels & toads & pencils
ink black   red   turquoise
(borrowed pen in math class)
skin   palm   fingertips
circle my wrist with green
leaves   red roses
draw a turquoise
bluebird on biceps
chain around ankle
heart locket in the pit
of my throat   half-moon
one star around navel
digging in   pen point
almost breaking through

pain   release   beauty

buried in the middle of the world

        here in the middle
           of the woods
           of arkansas
           of america

              buried
              in trash
          in the middle of the middle
              of the world

i need to find some solid ground
i need to find someone to believe
i need to run
run down the road     away
find somebody like me/not like me
      me/not me

     somebody brave     somebody who can find boy
       somebody to protect him

      run

          away

              from here

            (me)

lannie lets her long church hair
        down at night
        braids it tight
        winds it round her head
        next morning sitting up in bed


she piles it high, a tower   a nest
        covers it with a white hairnet


on my seventeenth birthday
lannie keeps me home from school
        takes me to ladies' bible class
        so i can learn modesty


next day i pierce
        my eyebrow, streak
        my choppy brown hair
          lipstick red
             &
          black as coal

it's like a burn
hot & rough & pain

my pencil eraser
my own design
my upper thigh

rubbing till it's numb
till the skin burns
till the scar forms

tonight
i draw seven stars on my belly where nobody but me can see
& i wish    on    each    one    send    him    back    please

This morning Boy's back in his bed,
Lannie hollering "Thank the Lord!"


Uncle Daddy pulls Boy's big toe,
his gruff voice says:
                    "Up 'n at 'em, garbage's wastin'."


Mugs of black coffee in our hands,
we squeeze into the truck cab.

We don't look at each other, but
it's good to have him here,

close enough the heat from his body
warms me & means he's alive.

He don't say nothing
          about where he went
          or the bruises on his arms,
          scratch under his left eye.

"Boy, please don't go off again, not without taking me along."

He looks up from his notebook
          where he's drawing with his black pen.
He shows me the picture,
          a kind of robot-looking butterfly.
    "This here's a tattoo design.  I'm making it for you."

I work hard not to cry.

He looks back down & colors in a wing.
            "I ain't going nowhere."

Boy dares me
Why not? I say
over & over
till I have to prove
to my own self
I ain't scared
I can take it

if it hurts
oh well

the first needle
aches


through anklebone

sets
my teeth
on edge


one hundred
needle-bites


white heat


buzzing my brain


firefirefire-firefirefire-fire

ink & skin


nightmoth:  swollen angel

Uncle Daddy says:

nobody living
in my house
with a tattoo
& that god-awful hair
mortal sin
desecration
of the temple
of God

he & Lannie won't
allow me in
church no more

still make Boy go

Yelling comes first
stomping next     Uncle Daddy

& Lannie both
hollering at
Boy
something  about
defilement     defacing     drawing

something about pews
& rockets
in
hymnals     robots

in the Bible
          Uncle Daddy hauls off his belt

Boy ducks—
too
late—
belt snaps
across his cheek

but I say
          we're not going to have that

no more &
Lannie smacks me
upside the head

Boy & me
we look at
each other


ice

in our eyes

frost
covering the garbage lids—
cold garbage
still stinks


we're leaving

leave


leaf


lea


le


l


eave
ave
ve
aving
ving
ing


ng


g

& we go
on a moonlight path

    dancing
    dancing

        down the highway
        to hitch a ride away

            way

                down

                    the road

away
from Lannie & Uncle Daddy
to find Raynell & Jobe

where Lannie & Uncle Daddy
can't preach, can't hit—
find Raynell

where we belong

they can't preach or hit
us no more

we belong
away     from this trash

no more
stinking at school

away     from this trashy
life

in the dark of the night at the Vernal truck stop, neon-flashing, diesel-smelling, pit stop on a cross-country racetrack, we spot a guy looking milder than the rest, ask for a ride. onto the night highway walled with pines & little bright eyes, onto the highway, away. sleep finds us both, Boy first, then me, that old life & stink draining off my shoulders, my eyes rolling & drowsy till I finally give in. still dark out when the driver hits the brakes, tells us, "you're here"—city streetlight-stained orangey clouds, sirens, chilly night air. we walk off like we know where we are going. "don't look back," Boy says. "just go." we turn a corner & slip behind an alley dumpster overflowing with greasy pizza boxes & beer bottles, huddle together, catnap till dawn. I find an animal cracker tin & tuck it in my backpack. safe with the decoration place's phone number in my pocket, Boy & me study the weird names & cool pictures painted on the alley walls & I say, "we'll see Raynell again today."

*North Little Rock, Arkansas*

From a pay phone etched
with jagged numbers
on a graffiti-
sprayed brick wall we call
Trish's Home Décor,

our heads together,
listening for Jobe's voice,
but he isn't there.
When Jobe's sister says,
"Thought you knew they moved

last week. Jobe answered
a newspaper ad
for a St. Louis
brewery job, real
good overtime pay,"

a big empty hole
opens inside me—
Boy, too, I can tell.
She says she doesn't
know their forwarding

address or phone yet.
Boy & I wander
North Little Rock's streets
asking each other,
"Why didn't she call?"

"Doesn't Raynell know
she should have told us?"

"How will we ever
find her now?"

"What if
she doesn't want us?"

Next day, Boy has to call Trish's again,
hoping.  She says, "Welfare

called. Where are y'all?"  My nerves
light up & I whisper,

"Hang up," but Boy asks, "Why didn't
Raynell call us?"

Trish says, "Jobe called. I heard him
asking for you, then

telling Lannie the news." I go limp,
thankful Boy never

gives up. "Didn't those son of a guns tell
y'all?" she says.

Boy's smiling, hanging up while her faint
voice says,

"Where are y'all? Do you need any help?"

(coffee shop, waitress wanted)

Working late every night, don't know what Boy's up to, hope
he's not into any trouble, but anyway we're both getting
money to get out of here, get on the road to St. Louis. Todd,
a busboy here at Della's Café, lets us sleep on his floor. Boy
found us a couple of ratty old sleeping bags in the dumpster
out back, washed them in the bathtub, & hung them on the
fence. Every night he stays out later & tonight don't even
come back at all. It's already five in the morning & I'm
shaking-scared & crying. Todd wakes up, steps over me to the
window, opens it to the dank cold air, drinks some orange
juice from a carton he keeps out on the ledge. He kicks Boy's
empty sleeping bag, stoops down, puts his hand on my
shoulder, acts like he's sorry I'm crying, but turns me round
& sticks his bitter tongue in my mouth & goes to touching me
anywhere he wants. I wallop him. His nose bleeding down his
chin, he pushes me over, says I'd better take my stuff & get
out or he won't be responsible. I grab up my backpack &
Boy's & run like heck, in case Todd's going to stop bleeding &
try to catch up to me. Around the corner, I duck under a store

awning & hide by the door, its locked metal gate shut & yellowed CLOSED sign stuck on the glass with a plastic suction cup. It's pouring down cold rain now. I squat down to wait for Boy, hope he's coming this way. A puddle fills up where a chunk's out of the sidewalk, cars shine their headlights on the silvery wet street, shushing by, morning traffic starting up, people yawning & sipping from chunky travel cups. Tires splash an arc of drops over the curb. The puddle rocks & overflows. A shoe sloshes into it—Boy's. He looks at me just like he knew I was there waiting for him.

Boy tells me:


"Sissy, I know where there's an empty house with a broken
back window.  If nobody else is using it, we can be safe
there, I bet.  At least we won't get wet."

He takes me down a hilly street to a house at the end,
makes a step for me out of his two hands & we scramble
inside a kitchen where painted names & gang signs splash
the walls & floor.  We find a closet under the stairs, shut
the door, & sleep, wet & smelling like old dogs.

Everything's fine

till I wake up

late in the afternoon in pitch black

shaking with this image in my mind's eye:

my clay woman

& Boy's paints in the old cigar box

still there under Todd's dresser

& with them, shining in the half-light,

my animal cracker tin

filled with every cent

we'd saved to get us to St. Louis.

Thunder crashing around him, Boy sets out to get our treasures.

He'll be soaked if he makes it back safe. *If.* Why did I say *if*?

I'm not sure where I am or how to find him if he gets caught.

I'm alone.      All alone.      In the lightning & thunder & rain.

A rustle in the bushes & I duck in case it's not Boy.

When I peek out, no one's there. No one. Just thunder
                                        lightning      rain.

Todd's probably home
from work     or soon
will be     I have to
go help Boy     have to
climb out the window

in the dark rain

Todd's door creaks open
& I creep inside
the twilight kitchen,

bump into Boy, right
inside the door, jump
clear out of my skin.

Heart booms; knees shake.
Boy hands me a garbage
bag & we take off.

finally


everything's




  . . . going to be
      . . . all right


(still a little out of breath    my heart beats heavy & steady
tension drains away    but not yet gone    we watch
the bus station door    in case Todd    barefoot    his hair on
end    that crazy look in his eyes    comes in & spots us)


  . . . now



everything's
    . . . ready
    . . . tied on our backs
        tickets for St. Louis
          in our hands

sweaty   leaving Little Rock
I take a birdbath

in the bus lavatory
eat Fritos & bean dip

we bought at the snack bar
lean my seat back

count stars through
my window   Boy falls fast

asleep   but I can't sleep
morning breaks & St. Louis's

silver arch shines like
dawn on red bricks

spray-painted names:
*GRAAT   ZELLZ   ARCHER*

huge jagged letters
across railroad bridges

water towers & billboards
graffiti blooms

lights up
Boy's eyes

*St. Louis, Missouri*

I dial information, get told the number, call
Raynell. She answers after just one ring

& next thing we know Jobe's driving
their van through the parking lot. Raynell

jumps out, grabs us, holds us tight, says,
"Where have you two been? You had us worried."

She smells good, just like herself, like
home. Jobe wraps us three in his arms

all warm & safe. Kylie, strapped in her seat,
reaches her little hands toward us & we

climb in already begging them not to tell
Welfare & Jobe says, "We'll take care of you.

You're home." Raynell pulls us up the stairs
telling about Jobe's job. In their apartment,

Boy helps Jobe move Kylie's little bed
into their one bedroom. In the living

room, Raynell & I make up the couch
for me, unfold a cot for Boy. Raynell's

homemade vegetable soup warms us & we
stay up late talking & laughing. Kylie

falls asleep in my lap sucking her thumb.
Boy says later whispering into the dark:

> *where Raynell is that's where it's home*

still a month to go before summer vacation   Raynell enrolls
us in the high school & we get set up in classes  with books
titled   *algebra in everyday life   our english language*   &
*the solar system & you*   mostly    they make us write all
the time      Boy says he likes it because they let him write
song lyrics & say they're poems    say to him    *you are
a born poet*    but we like our art classes best   Boy learns
about painting pictures with words in them    he puts in
a poem & makes friends of the teacher   I have a clay class &
all I can think to make is a terra-cotta woman with her hands
outstretched  round clumps of clay stuck on her fingers
when she comes out of the bisque fire I paint blue   white &
green glaze on the clumps   & promise her shiny little worlds
at her fingertips

evenings
at home we
>      study
>      watch TV
>      play cards
like a party
all the time
till Boy says
we got to help

somehow
>      get summer jobs
>      take care of Kylie

summer heat
coming on & we
>      stop playing
>      get crowded
>      sweat in front of a box fan

evening sun
pounds Raynell
cooking supper
I help & try to learn

Boy & Kylie
take a walk
to cool her
so she can sleep

Boy & I look for work
            after school
get out from underfoot
            at night
even if Raynell says
she worries when
we're late
we tell her we just want to visit
our friends & she says
she remembers how that is—
just be careful

first     Boy finds Tyrone in art class
   then    I find Dolores in math
now    we all hang
     together


they say    "urban art"
  they say    "we can teach you"
      & they do
      & we are set


we love it
     we laugh
         & run—art bandits

school's out
get ready for

summer nights
game time

playing tag
with cops—

climb fences
spray-paint

run, scramble
over tracks

down ladders
up fire

escapes     black
clothes     gloves

knit caps—
Tyrone says

artists should
be free

art should
rage over

every blank
wall     every

train car—
Boy & Tyrone

Dolores & me
paint worlds

turn rust
to silver

& brick
to gold

Boy loves every plan
sketches maps in his piecebook
scouts out buildings
sneaks out late
          at night
goes alone
until
he tells me, "You need to practice."


from Jobe & Raynell's second-floor apartment
we sneak up back stairs to a third-floor
ladder & out a roof hatch

under the stars we leap

roof to roof
buildings almost touching
travel a block
turn
run
two more roofs

& spray concrete
block wall
almost done & a head
juts from a window
mouth yells "Call the police" & we run

back across roofs I try to be quiet
but breath pants & heart
pounds & feet
clatter
sirens coming
we dive the hatch
scramble stairs &
tiptoe
click Jobe & Raynell's front door
locked behind us

in our beds
dark living room
sirens pass by
& we're
safe

Boy can't get enough
I ask "What if we get caught?"
He says "We won't."

With Tyrone & Dolores
we creep down
alleys spray

dumpsters & back doors
fences & walls
spray high as

we can reach
whisper & follow
hide & run

crawl over boxcars
dangle from ladders
one-handed

whisper & laugh
Tyrone & Dolores
say we're ready

to climb but I ask
"What about falling?"
Tyrone says

"Always have a plan.
Watch your step
& test ladders

before you climb."
Dolores says, "Look
out for dark sky

lights & air shafts
& never go blindly
into the shadows."

Kylie
Three years old now
Holds out her hands to Boy
Jumps up & down, says, "Dance me, Boy."
They dance.

Summer:
We babysit.
Raynell works days, Jobe nights
I work afternoons, Boy mornings.
I cook.

Boy mows
Lawns. Kylie helps
Make tomorrow's lunches.
We put on tonight's dinner then
We play.

At noon
She naps. I leave
When Boy gets home & walk
Two blocks to Sonic where I serve
Fast food.

Some days
Garbage trucks leak
Sour juice by the dumpsters
Then just looking at food makes me
Feel sick.

After
Twilight we leave
Jobe, Raynell, & Kylie
So they can have time alone &
We run.

We climb
The city, dance
St. Louis, sing & love
St. Louie, run & paint & own
Our city.

we name ourselves
dancing in paint

float on fumes
urban ocean spray

high we float
over riverboat casinos

higher than ourselves
name each other

above dark bridges
tiny twinkly lights

old rolling river
rolling through us

like we're old
as that river

& nothing can
ever touch us

Boy's eyes
how they do shine
catch the starlight
beam it back

I want to say
I love you, brother
want to hear
I love you, too

we won't break
night's silence
but we both know
we know

best of the best: *(like maybe this could be home)*

ARCHER

ZELLZ

&

GRAAT

highest names in St. Louis  *(we feel good about St. Louis)*
no one knows their real names
like caped crusaders
& masked invaders

like we are now
our crew          *(with Jobe & Raynell & Kylie)*
Dolores is

&
Tyrone

&
*(seeing our names higher &)*

Boy is

his colors black & blue
& turquoise when he can get it     *(wears the crown & all)*
I go by

I spray my name gold & red
intensify with black
permanent marker   makes     *(at least they know your name)*
it look deep & important

we feel good about St. Louis     *(we've always wanted a name)*
like maybe it could be home
with Jobe & Raynell & Kylie
walking around town every day &
seeing our names higher


                              *(zellz & graat & archer)*
& higher in the city   we try to go

higher than anybody   whoever
climbs highest wins          *(giving intensity to it)*



wears the crown & all
the painters know you—
& maybe so do the cops—
at least they know your name



                    *(atenz*
                         *his colors are black & blue)*

all taggers want the arch
whoever

        owns the arch
        owns the city

name above it
name on the march
    like Lewis & Clark
    through the gateway to the west blazed
    across deserts & grain

        & purple mountain's majesties

        you see your tag
in daylight    you know
        you have a home

city after midnight
creeping in shadows
        design memorized
I'm carrying red

& gold    Tyrone    green & yellow
        Boy    black & blue
Dolores—the watcher
        city night sounds

        siren in the distance
hope they're not
        coming our way
we're bombing

tonight—an old wooden
        water tank atop
an ancient warehouse
        Tyrone planned for days

        scouted    sketched
divided into sections
        Boy & Tyrone
test the fire escape

bolted to bricks
        oil gears
pull-down stairs
        so quiet in the dark

                    our sneakers' muffled tapping
up the zigzag escape
                    reach the warehouse roof
Boy & Tyrone

with me right behind
                    climb the water tank's
ladder    rickety old wood
                    splintering down in my face

                    one more step &
Boy's almost there
                    ladder creaks
water tank shifts

leans toward us    we scramble
                    down fast as we can
Dolores signals a low whistle
                    somebody's coming

                    we run away across the roof
tower leaning     behind us
                    metal hitting concrete
Tyrone goes over the side

his head pops back up
                    to show us the way
to a ladder or another roof
                    Boy looks back at me

makes sure I'm with them
& leaps the low wall
        about a yard to Tyrone's right
he disappears     screaming

Tyrone yells     "oh man!"
        Dolores & I follow
him down the ladder
        he's been standing on

        till we're hovering over Boy
in the flashlight spill
        all broken & bloody
his wide-open eyes

search for mine
        "Boy!" I'm yelling
holding him
        hearing his breath

        & his moans
moaning with him
        I ask     "why didn't you look?"
it wasn't on the plan

we're supposed to look
        light spots us & a cop
shouts     "oh my god
        call the paramedics!"

    & somebody comes
up behind us    Dolores
     & Tyrone run away
just after Boy stops breathing

 the medics start working on him
       right there    take him away
strapped to a gurney
     following them I ask

     "why didn't you look?"
we weren't supposed to
     jump into the dark
we weren't supposed to fall

i fight

all elbows      knees & spit

but      she gets handcuffs

on me in nothing flat

won't let me ride with Boy

    won't even let me cry


shoves me into her squad car


i say      "but he's my brother"

she says      "shut up, kid"

    i shut up


    i can't breathe

judge says    "crime against property
assault       on an officer of the law"


Jobe's there
his face

gray as
jail walls

Boy?
so still

Raynell?
holding

Boy's
hand


*my own recognizance*:
      released only for the funeral
   then Missouri Youth Center
      four months' sentence

during the service

as if from far away        i watch Raynell
watch tears        run down her face
    run over her chin        see
    how she wipes her neck
            shuts her eyes        grieves
                she's letting him go        *how can she do that?*


                i vow my tears won't
let him go        i won't cry
        tears of release  i won't ever
        let him go into my grief

after the pallbearers carry Boy out
Jobe soothes Raynell

she says
"I should have watched over him"

she looks at me     says
"We should have watched out for him"

they hug me goodbye
could i have kept him safe?

*my own recognizance*:
   at night now

all i can hear:

      Boy

      his scream             the sound

                   of

      his body             breaking

all i can see:

      his eyes      searching      for me

it hits me like this every morning:


he's gone, him still Boy,
just a boy, never a man,
never with a wife or kid,


*see how he danced*
*round & round the rosie*
*with Kylie, see how*
*they laughed, do you*
*see what you lost?*
*do you?*

can't draw on skin
     with a stubby pencil

         no jewelry, no makeup—
         just a blue shirt
         & pants to match,

            like hospital clothes
            on TV

plastic
forks & spoons

try to slice
BBQ ribs with a spoon

no plastic knives
for safety's sake

mostly it's spaghetti
& tiny meatballs

that look like cat food
& smell like garbage

short yellow jail pencils
no erasers
no forgiveness
    when you make a mistake
    X it out
        or learn to be
        neat
        cleaned up
        reformed

Once a week
Raynell visits me.
We don't talk
about Boy.

She sits with me
as long as she can,
but about Boy,
neither of us can speak.

As long as she can
she keeps from crying.
Neither of us can speak
the words, "He's gone."

She keeps from crying
& i tell her about classes,
the words *He's* & *gone*
always in my eyes.

i tell her about my classes,
& she says, try to get the GED.
Always in my eyes,
behind my eyes, Boy's face.

She says, "Try to get your GED
Don't waste your time in here"—
behind my eyes, Boy's face—
"Who knows how much time a person has?"

If i don't waste my time here,
if i can say his name
or care how much time there is
maybe i can find a way to live.

If Raynell could say his name
once this week,
maybe she could find a way to live,
but still we don't talk.

G.E.D.—great effin' diploma
& i'm not stupid enough
to think i don't need it
sometimes i think
i should just fail
everything
what's
that
about?

> (i know i don't deserve a good life if Boy can't have one
>> i know
>> i can't ever serve enough time
>>> work enough bad jobs)


>>> but i pass the test
>>> i get the effin' diploma

freedom


yeah, right

Sure i can walk around
anywhere i want, all
over the city, sure i can
but without Boy, why?

At Jobe & Raynell's
we sit watching TV,
watching Kylie play
Totsee Toys, listen

how she makes them
talk to each other
& she calls one of them
Boy, then stops &

looks at us & pipes
up, craning her neck,
singing out, "Boy-eeee,
c'mere. See my story."

Raynell whispers to me,
"We tried to explain
what death is, but she
pretends he's still here,

in the bathroom or gone
to work. When we say
he isn't coming back,
she puts her finger up

& hushes us." Kylie
looks at me & says,
"Sissy came back.
Let's wait for Boy."

i want      to be      like Kylie      believing      in Boy      alive
when      Raynell or Jobe      try again      to teach her about      death
i leave      go      sit on the roof      play over      our last night
like a tape      in my mind      it loops round      & back      & starts
over again      & Boy      falls      then runs to the edge      again      falls
screaming into night      then runs to the edge again & i yell stop
but still he falls      screams come from all of us:      cops & kids
& Boy                  & then                  he's quiet


i want      when      i leave      like a tape      over again      screaming
but still he falls      to be      Raynell & Jobe  go      in my mind
& Boy falls      into night      screams      like Kylie      try again
sit on the roof      it loops round      then runs to the edge      then
runs to the edge again      from all of us:      cops & kids & Boy
believing in      to teach her about      play over      & back      again
&      & then      Boy      alive      our last night      & starts      falls
i yell                  stop                  he's quiet


he's quiet      & then      cops & kids & Boy      runs to the edge
screams      stop      i yell      & back again      from all of us:
it loops round      then falls      into night      & Boy      play over
& starts      to teach her about      our last night      to the edge again
sit on the roof      in my mind      go      like a tape      Raynell &
Jobe      like Kylie      try again      when i leave      over again
i want      Boy alive      believing      & then runs      in      screaming
to be                  but still he falls                  falls

"come with us,"
Raynell begs.
Jobe holds her

hand. "Jobe's lost
his job. we'll
go back home."

"home?" i say.
"do you mean
Lexieville?

no, Raynell,
where Boy is
that's my home."

Why don't they know I can't leave Boy's grave?
All my memories are him & me
playing, teasing, napping. I remember
sharing all our joys & all our pain.
For me where Boy is, is where it's home,
this place where he could choose & paint his name.

My brother always wanted a real name.
**Boy Lexie** looks so sad carved on his grave,
the stone so small & gray; now it's his home
& i am left with no one, only me
to fight the loneliness & all this pain,
to be the only one remembering

our Boy—unless night itself remembers
how he saw its face & called its name
& danced inside its smoke & wore its pain.
He left me here to haunt his early grave,
to learn the dance the night has saved for me,
to dance & dance & dance till i find home.

i wonder if i'd recognize my home
back in Arkansas. What i remember
bleeds into all my dreams: just Boy & me
& trash. Here Atenz was his chosen name
so tomorrow when i visit Boy's grave
i'll spray-paint **Atenz RIP**, my pain

a stream of black & gold & turquoise paint,
& then across the arch, **_You're finally home_**.
For my headstone i'll have someone engrave
"Sissy loved her brother & remembered
his name forever." i'll keep his tag name
a lifelong secret between him & me.

As soon as he could walk he followed me
around the house & he was such a pain;
when he got hurt he'd cry & squeal my name
& i would wipe his tears & lead him home
for Raynell to rock. Will he remember
how we loved him if i desert his grave?

Raynell & Jobe begged me to go home,
said I'm too grave & much too filled with pain
to live alone remembering his name.

i'm staying
with Dolores    though
her mama says    only

   a couple of days
when they kick me out
Dolores goes too &

we wander    down-
town till       we find
a warehouse          with a river

view    near that shiny silver
arch    low-rent
district        broken

windows    no heat & not
   too many druggies
shoving needles    up

their veins   & puking
their guts out
                on the floor

i keep looking, every night, all over town,

read new graffiti    crazy hoping maybe

i'll see a new **atenz** on a new wall     i get so lost

step    step    splash    wet pavement    muddy grass

boot top splashed    mud    mud    rain    running down

my neck    in my eyes    keep on    on-on-on-on

past the sandwich sign    neon ice-cream-cone-light

grease-frying-exhaust from the alley    somebody's cell

phone trilling on the corner    somebody's voice


in the night


but not Boy's

forgetting

is not that

easy

getting for-
gotten
is

        when it rains
        mist covers
        where we sleep

                  kids
               cough
                 all night

     shadows move from corner to stair
     next day someone else is
     gone

who?

                     I forget

Dolores wakes in the middle
of the night, sits up
& calls my name, *Skye,*
she whispers & shakes
my arm, punches my
side & says, *Listen!*

*Wake up & listen*
*to that middle-*
*aged crazy man, my*
*God—something's up*
& Dolores shakes
me & whispers *Skye!*

*Wake up, wake up. Skye,*
*you better listen*
& Dolores shakes
me from the middle
of my dream, wakes up
all of us in my

sleeping corner, my
only friends. *Hey, Skye,*
*you better wake up.*
*Sit up & listen.*
*You're in the middle-*
*aged man's dream!* She shakes

so hard laughing, shakes
me, keeps on till my
head clears. The middle-
aged man cries out, *Sky
is falling, listen
people, listen up!*

*You better wake up
before the earth shakes
& dissolves, listen,
beloved, to my
warning!  No more sky,
nothing!*  The crazy middle-

aged man sits up & shakes his fist
at the sky, then at me & my friends
listening, delirious, in the middle of the night.

next morning   crazy man's gone   no one remembers
        laughing at him
no one remembers his dream   remembers delirium
        dissolving earth   falling sky
crazy man   *so who's crazy now?*   i ask Dolores & she says
        now she remembers
says   *i think i've had about enough of this i miss my mother*
        *& brothers*   i say
*you are so lucky   & you don't even know it   you don't owe*
        *me a thing   go home*


it doesn't matter     anyway                *the sky is falling*
i'm alone without Boy     anyway             *sky is falling*
now no one i know ever met Boy                *i'm falling*
no one knows what we have lost                 *falling*

*d*
*-i*
*-s*
*-s*
*-o*
*-l*
*-v*
*-e:*

*to become one*
*with the surrounding matter*
*so as to become undetectable*
*as a separate entity*
*by the ordinary means of the senses*

we   run   we   paint   we   laugh   we   drink   we   keep out
        we   trespass

                                              & we go
                                              nowhere

we   cry   we   drink   we   sleep   we . . .   till   there's
        no one
                                                      but me

i     cry     i     drink     i     sleep     i     drink     i     cry
        till     dark

&   somebody cares     somebody feeds me
        somebodytouchesme     some
                              body

when i wake up,
nobody knows where
dolores has gone

nobody knows
who i'm talking
about    nobody knows

*dolores*    you know
i say    but when
i look close

i don't know them
& i've lost time
lost myself

in a bottle    lost
days & nights
& dolores gone home

jobe & raynell
gone home
when i wake up

the


sad
way

light
falls

across
glass

sooty
streaky

rain
stained

panes
between

dreams
&

me

dreams?
&
me?


what about boy?     what
about his dreams?     *what*
*were your dreams?     boy*
*i don't know—     did you*
*plan to climb &     paint &*
*run all your life?     did you*
*want to end up here     like me?*


icicles break sunlight     colors
dirty windows break     rainbows
break on the floor     broken
dirty icicles break     spill
sunlight's beauty &     melt
why do our dreams     die?

*can you smell it? (i say)*
what? (he says)

*what we're eating (i say)*
what are we eating? (he says)

*looks like maybe*
*fried chicken or fish (i say)*

soggy hush puppies (he says)
*limp french fries (i say)*

hoo-ha! found a packet
half-full of ketchup (he says)

*can you taste it? (i say)*
what?

ketchup? (he says)
*tastes kind of funny (i say)*

ha-ha—hear me laughing (he says)
*shut up (i say)*

hey! watch your mouth (he says)
*somebody's coming (i say)*

hide. . . . (he says)
*shut the dumpster (i say)*

they gone? (he says)
*open the lid*

*let me out! (i say)*
now i smell it (he says)

*i can't eat this (i say)*
wait—here's a biscuit

with gravy! (he says)

i wrap newspapers inside my denim jacket
for warmth     find a pair of somebody's
left-behind boots     too big     but warm

pull my knit cap down low & walk through
sunshine     squinting     huddled inside
myself     to boy's grave     i am the only

visitor here     BOY LEXIE it says     carved
sharp in stone     BOY LEXIE     *if you were*
*anywhere   why would you be here?   would you*

*go to   Rome     Egypt     Athens? i know*
*you would have gone far     as soon as*
*you were able     as soon as i'd let go*

now     i can't let go     &     i can't go

his headstone
a mountain
he's gone
beyond
i can't see him
can't remember
his face
imagine dull
dead eyes
yes
but that isn't Boy
my Boy shines
he fell & broke
into pieces
icicles melt
rainbows
dissolve
people
die *why*
*you?*
i am the only
visitor here
i yell                              "Boy! Why didn't you look?"

*Boy*
*you never drew escape paths    in your plans*
*never even looked for them    why didn't you*
*think we could get caught?    why didn't you*
*know someone could die    you could die?*

*you are still a pain     i can't get away from*
*you*     i grab his stone & push it     pull it
try to shake it     *don't you know     i don't*
*know what to do without you?     i'll never . . .*

                              "Boy! Do you hear me?"

forgive you for leaving me     never
overhead thin ice clouds
frozen tree limbs don't
move i am the only
thing moving i
pound stone
throat hurts
hands ache
such cold
stone
i am
th
e


        o


             n




                   l




                        y

even so   i        forgive              rise up

                    &      leave

          his       grave      leave   Boy's      grave

(i am the only one here)

i walk past the school not worried about getting recognized but Dolores leaving with some boy sees me crossing the street sees me in the ratty old clothes i dug out of an EARTHRIGHT collection bin sees how i've wrapped myself in newspapers & wear floppy men's boots without laces sees & frowns looks away & walks off with that boy but when i'm halfway down the block she's running up beside me handing me a twenty saying here says she owed it to my brother & for a second she goes to hug me but pulls back before she has to touch me "girl you got to pull yourself together what would Boy say if he could see you now?" i smell myself then & tears roll out & down sting my chapped face she says Raynell calls her house all the time asking for me Raynell still loves me she runs back to that boy & i hold Boy's warm money tight in my cold fist i need to buy paint—black & gold & turquoise

$10 worth of spray paint &
i imagine
he's with me
& Boy & me paint
his name all over this city

next morning i walk
right up to a drive-in
window, order a breakfast
sandwich & a frosty
chocolate shake & pay for it—
tastes so real i think
i'm dreaming

at the warehouse
there's nobody to feel

ashamed in front of
only myself to care

about myself     nobody
tells me one thing

to do or not & i can't
see inside these faces

blank eyes     warped
mouths     gambling

life away     not
a chance     no

hope until someone
paints a wall black

adds a turquoise
sea & golden

galaxies & that
          somebody is

          me

I find
        more paint
                in an art studio's

dumpster
        now I have
                a painted-on bed

chair & lamp
        sunflowers spilling
                across the wall

above my head
        while I sleep
                I give everybody

the room of their
        dreams     a tent     a mansion
                an igloo     the Taj Mahal

& I ask their names
        (Annie     Oscar     Luis
                Old Mel)     &

tell them about Boy
        & sometimes they
                cry with me

an artist's studio
with a mountain view
I paint on back of Boy's
gravestone imagine him
laughing being happy
climbing mountains
instead of walls

I imagine Boy
running with me
all over

St. Louis,
giving every
neighborhood

a midnight mural:
Van Gogh's room
on a deli wall

downtown,
the Alps
over the high-

school gym
in Kirkwood,
an apple orchard

on Applebee's.
Boy & me
paint the world

& we love
this painted world
& all our colors.

Beside the dumpster in the studio alley, it shines
up at me, colorful & barely crumpled,
not even dirty, a brochure with photos of artwork,
photos of students, of easels & potters' wheels,
heavy portfolios, bearded & longhaired professors
pointing to pictures of haystacks, paragraphs
on graduation requirements, graduation
exhibits, job opportunities, art history,
the human form, advanced design, beginning life
drawing, mixed media, display & framing techniques,
senior class show, intermediate perspective,
collage & found objects, a view to the future
      & you, too, can be a part of it, part of the world of art,
      of an ancient lineage, the family of the arts—in Chicago.


Through touristy Laclede's Landing down by the river,
past the bars & cafés, I head back to the warehouse, crying
my eyes out. *That's where we should have gone*
*someday, Boy,* I whisper, *That's where*
*we can never go.*
I toss the brochure into a wire trash basket.
It sifts down to the bottom, still
keeping me in sight.
I turn away, go about a block, jazzy music out a door
stops me & I stare in at the laughing drinking people,
wonder if they need somebody to help out,
but I can't stand it.
      I dig that art school pamphlet from the trash,
      flick some old sticky paper off it, & take it away.

Next day, if I were to say, *Boy, should I show this to Annie or Luis or somebody?*

he might say, *Won't hurt nothing,* so I do.

They say, "Too bad your Boy ain't alive to go to that school, too bad. Too bad, too bad."

If I were to say, "Treasures in the trash,"
*Glories in the garbage,* Boy might add.

A dumpster behind a framing shop yields
glue & gesso, scraps of canvas & wood,

pasteboard boxes & dabs of paint to make
collages. From metal I make robot worlds

for Boy. I pretend Boy collects food
labels to paste in kaleidoscopic designs.

We sculpt new shapes from old boxes,
form new worlds from old trash. We laugh

& surprise ourselves with joy. I lift up
like I might float away.  Boy's not gone,

not as long as I remember.

Morning light shines on
the art school brochure.
Evening wishdreams:  Boy

painting a ceiling
& no need to fear,
paid instead of chased.

Night dreams:  I design
ancient mosaics
for a Roman wall,

set shards in plaster,
tap in a story
time won't erase, Boy

& me immortal.
Morning light—the art
school brochure—erase

those dreams, forget them,
if not for my own
sake, then for his.

(Give it up, Sissy
Get on with it, girl
Get a job & forget it
Give up)

but I can't—
down to the river to wash away my sins
wash away my crusty skin, the dust ground into my face
down to the river, to wash away my sorrows
wash away my hopes
ignore my dreams
but I can't

rinse out the old clothes, wash out my hair
sit in the sunshine to let it dry
hobble over the cobblestone streets barefooted
Laclede's Landing Big River Tavern, just loud enough
just quiet enough, just enough
dishwashing, garbage scraping
bringing scraps back
for supper

enough money to wash my clothes in a real washer
let them dry on the windowsill
buy a used pair of blue jeans & some dingy old shoes
wear a Big River Tavern T-shirt
now serving for tips, ask:
"are you still working on that?"  hope not & hope no
doggie bag, except for mine.  don't need to buy food
it's everywhere, a bit here, a bit there, no germs to speak of
not like real garbage

Telephone cold on my ear, I say, "Raynell, it's me." (Heart pounding)

She's crying saying my name & "Where have you been, are you all right?"

"I'm still here, working at Big River & yes, eating real good, yes, warm & safe place to sleep, living with new friends, doing fine, fine, how's Jobe & Kylie, any news about Mama?" (Tears)

"We're all fine, heard she'd been seen near Conway but who knows? Don't you worry about us, come on home, I'll send you money or come get you, whichever. . . ."

"No, I can't leave." (Coal in stomach)

"Sissy, you need us & we need you. I don't want to lose you again."

"No, I can't leave, not yet. Maybe someday. . . ." (Dizzy, almost hoping)

"How can I reach you?" (Tavern getting crowded)

"Leave a message here at work & I'll get it at my next shift. Got to go. Another of my table's just been sat." (Got to go)

By the time I bring fried catfish to the next table,

my throat won't even work to ask,    "Need anything else?"

for needing Raynell,    wishing I could leave,    knowing
                                                    I shouldn't

Prying open oysters for hours

Sunday Brunch special, slimy creatures,

never a pearl no matter how much

you believe.

Protein at the Big River Tavern:
(Proteins, the building blocks of life)

> To eat an oyster raw
> you salt it, lemon juice &
> sauce it, don't look
> at it, have a saltine
> ready—slide the glob
> onto tongue, bite
> corner off cracker,
> chew two or three times,
> crunch helps hide the slime,
> peppers make you swallow
> fast, chase it with something
> strong & citrusy, a few good
> gulps & never, ever
> eat them straight
> from the garbage.

Bewhiskered catfish heads
you chop off with a wide
flat blade. (Mr. Chang, the cook,
tells about fish head soup
a delicacy—fish head soup!)
Slice the belly open, gut
it, scale it, fillet out the fine
sharp backbone, dip in batter,
& fry it up with hush puppies,
nothing else like it on the Big
Rolling River. But mostly
leftovers go home
for the doggies.

After midnight, Mr. Chang
finishes his soup,
sits down to eat, gives
me a bowl, hot & soothing—
all I'll have for my dinner.
He waits till I nod
& we sit quiet, tired,
waiting for the last
table to leave,
thankful for all
the little fishes.

Light from the street
haloes around her
when she opens the door
Just like in a cowboy show

stranger rides in     slams
through the saloon's
swinging doors & all
hell breaks loose     Nothing's

ever the same again
Whole town changes     Sometimes
somebody dies like Boy
died     sudden & too soon

But sometimes somebody
might get brought back
to life     like me
right now

watching Raynell spot me
& come running     arms wide
& tears spilling down     Sometimes
when a person can't find

her home     her home
finds her     Weeping
we hug & rock each other
& I almost hear Boy's words

from when we first arrived
at Raynell & Jobe's door—
*Where Raynell is
that's where it's home*

We sit & talk & Raynell soaks in my voice
& I soak in hers. We laugh. She asks
me what I want to do. "I have no choice,"
I say, I'll learn the skills to do the tasks
to keep this job & stay, but when I show
her the brochure she says that I should move
to Chicago, but could I up & go
& leave Boy here alone?  "Raynell, I love
that dream, but I can't. I'm not that brave."
Raynell smiles & says, "If Boy could,
he'd go with you, but now you have to save
your own life & honor his. You should
go. If you could ask Boy what to do,
he'd say to go. Chicago. You should go."

"Jobe said tell you we never

     should have let you go
     to all them foster homes.
     We should've hung on tight
     & never let you go.

     But if you want to go
     to art school, take this cash
     we saved for your way home
     & go to Chicago.

Sissy, remember this:

     No matter where you go,
     you have a home with Jobe
     & me, always. Our love
     will never let you go."

Thrift store backpack
on my back,
shoes & clothes

we bought yesterday,
Raynell & I
march toward Amtrak,

cross Union Station
& restaurant smells
mingle with fountains'

misty spray &
her train goes
south & mine

will go north.
We wave farewell,
not goodbye.

Now I'm alone,
but not lonely,
holding my own

real family deep
inside my own
beating heart, whether

living or gone:
Jobe, Kylie, Raynell,
Boy & me.

*Chicago, Illinois, Sissy Lexie, age 18*


Train
creaks out of the St. Louis station,
rocking us like Raynell used to do.
I ask Boy, *What would you do if you was me?*

With his sweet voice trailing off, almost
lost in the train's lonely whistle
Boy might whisper:

> *I'd go    Sissy    go*
> > *to    Chicago    with    you*

> > > > *Chi—*
> > > > > *ca—*
> > > > > > *go—*


Train
packed with people, babies crying
foil-wrapped fried chicken
languages I've never heard before
      even English in new shapes

In Chicago, skyscrapers
rise like stars
rise like bridges to the night
planets & universes
      of light

Someday I'll be up there
    looking down
    at some girl getting off a train

    I promise Boy:

        *Someday*

            *some*

                *day. . . .*

*Chicago, Skye Lexie, today*


I put on long yellow rubber gloves for the Chicago back-alley
    garbage bins


every time I open a dumpster I recall Lannie's wading boots
        & think I should buy some

but I never do
       maybe


           one of these days
           I'll open a lid
           & find a pair


now I know

I can find anything
      I want—


           half-used spray-paint cans
           plus
                 aerosol deodorant tips
                 art markers & grease pens
                 = Atenz wildstyle all over this city

coffee shop jobs
& cleaning up after receptions
= something to eat

Grant Park in the summer
& friends in the winter
= a place to sleep


smashed soda cans
plus
      twisted baby dolls
      broken tiles & jars
      = collage
        like
financial aid & promises
      = college

Cast-off jewelry
I take apart,
bead hair clips

(like Lou), glue
rhinestones on shoes
(like Mama wore),

sell (like Lannie)
or use (like
Raynell) until it's

all used up.
(Like Mr. Chang
saved fish heads)

I gather beads—
to feed my
hungry art—faceted

& luminous, string
into ropes &
hang on my

art school's walls,
pearly loops, haloed
rainbows of silken

light, shining (like
Boy) on black
robocopters & velvet-

winged nightmoths
suspended by threads
invisible but (like

Skye Lexie) strong
enough to hold.

I visit Raynell        or she visits me        once a year at least

but (Boy might say)

*like a downhill stream*
          *you can't go back*
                    *only forward*

*these days*  (Boy might also say)

*one woman's trash*
*is another woman's*
*one-woman show*

          *Boy*
                    (I'd say back)

                    *who'd ever imagine*

                    *I'd come to love*

                              *all     this     trash?*

**SHARON DARROW** taught at an arts and media college on an urban Chicago campus, where instead of ivy halls, grassy quads, and tree-lined paths, her students walked through graffiti-lined streets and rode elevators to classrooms where passengers on the "L" peered in the windows to wave at the young poets at work. Some of the students also danced, rapped, made movies, or photographed their world, and some were art students by day, graffiti artists by night. Their stories inspired these poems.

When Sissy and Boy Lexie first appeared, they were young children in her novel *The Painters of Lexieville.* When they appeared again as teenage foster kids, they had become artists, and Sharon Darrow knew she and they were in for a great adventure. Her books, *Old Thunder and Miss Raney, Through the Tempests Dark and Wild,* and *The Painters of Lexieville,* are all about strong young women who triumph in the face of adversity. *Trash* is her first book of poems and her second book for young adults. She enjoys teaching writing and admires the grit, beauty, innovation, and courage she sees in young poets' and artists' work today. Sharon Darrow lives and teaches in Vermont.